OPERATION PHOTOBOMB

Tara Luebbe &
Becky Cattie

illustrated by
Matthew Rivera

Albert Whitman & Company
Chicago, Illinois

HA CASS COUNTY PUBLIC LIBRARY
400 E. MECHANIC
HARRISONVILLE, MO 64701

0 0022 0572823 7

To Stacy McAnulty, my mentor and friend—TL
To our brother Josh, the original prankster—BC
For Mom and Dad. Thank you for a lifetime of love and support—MR

Library of Congress Cataloging-in-Publication data is on file with the publisher.

Text copyright © 2019 by Tara Luebbe and Becky Cattie
Illustrations copyright © 2019 by Matthew Rivera
First published in the United States of America in 2019 by Albert Whitman & Company
ISBN 978-0-8075-6130-0 (hardcover)
ISBN 978-0-8075-6129-4 (ebook)

All rights reserved. No part of this book may be reproduced or transmitted in any
form or by any means, electronic or mechanical, including photocopying,
recording, or by any information storage and retrieval system,
without permission in writing from the publisher.

Printed in China
10 9 8 7 6 5 4 3 2 1 HH 24 23 22 21 20 19

Design by Morgan Beck

For more information about Albert Whitman & Company,
visit our website at www.albertwhitman.com.

100 Years of Albert Whitman & Company
Celebrate with us in 2019!

Monkey and Chameleon loved jungle tours.
Jungle tours meant new toys.

"Look what I got!"
said Monkey.

"Lucky you—
I only got this junk,"
said Chameleon.

At first, Monkey was all thumbs. But after
he got the hang of it, he ran to show his pals.
"Everyone get together. Squish in."

CLICK!

"Take another one of me," said Chameleon.
"Not yet," said Monkey.
"This picture is only for the birds."

CLICK!

"This time, just animals with fur."

CLICK!

Then Chameleon had a picture-perfect idea.
He waited for just the right moment...

"Photobomb!"

CLICK!

"Chameleon, please
don't do that!"

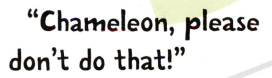

But Chameleon was just getting started.

Capybara's
family portrait.
"Photobomb!"

CLICK!

Sloth's new
baby photos.
"Photobomb!"

CLICK!

And Grandpa Macaw's 76th birthday pictures. "Photobomb!"

CLICK!

"Help me stop him from wrecking all the pictures!" Monkey howled.

Toucan tried to distract him.
"Photobomb!"

CLICK!

Jaguar tried to be tricky.
"Photobomb!"

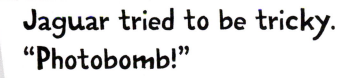

CLICK!

The tapirs tried to block him.
"Photobomb!"

CLICK!

"Stop it!"
Monkey screeched.
"Stop it! Stop it! STOP IT!"

"That picture was for family only!"

"You scared my baby!"

"You crashed my party!"

"Fine." Chameleon said.
"You won't see me in any more pictures."

But then the animals noticed something. "Is that...?"

CHAMELEON!

"There must be a way to stop that wily whippersnapper," said Grandpa Macaw.

"I have an idea," said Monkey. "Huddle up."

Finally, they had it: a perfect plan. Operation Photobomb was a go.

"NOW it's your turn, Chameleon," said Monkey.

Chameleon struck a pose.

"Can you scoot over a tiny bit to the left? Perfect."
Monkey counted. "1...2...3..."

"Bombs away!" the macaws yelled.

SPLAT!

CLICK!

"Now *that's* a photobomb!"
squawked Grandpa Macaw.

"Stop laughing! It's not funny!"
said Chameleon.

"You ruined my pic...Ohhhhh!"

"Truce?" asked Monkey.

"Truce," agreed Chameleon.

Monkey went back to his hobby.

But Chameleon kept his promise and did not go back to his.

Bah!

CLICK!

CLICK!

Awk!

Mmph!

CLICK!

Then **Chameleon** had a picture-perfect idea. He waited for just the right **moment**...

"PHOTOBOMB!"